Places in the United States

by Mary Taylor

HOUGHTON MIFFLIN   BOSTON

We live in the United States. Some people call it the U.S.A.

The United States is a big country. It has many places. It has lots of people.

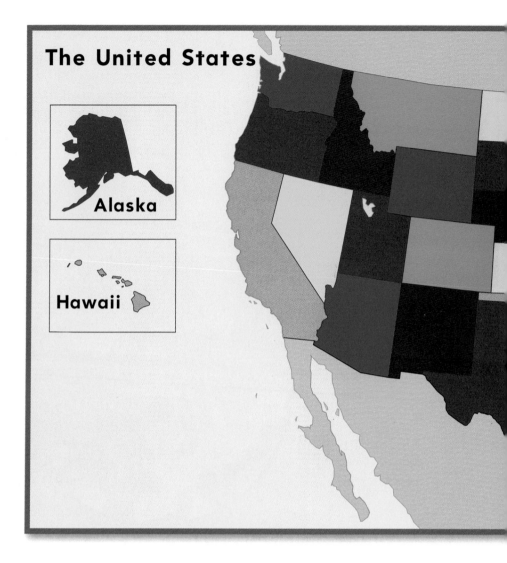

The United States

Alaska

Hawaii

This is a map of the United States.

The United States has 50 states. Look at the shapes. The states are all on the map.

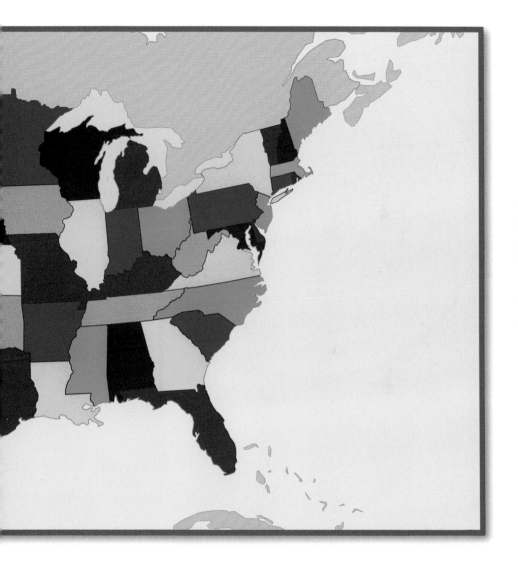

Your state is on this map too. What is the name of your state? Do you think you can find it on the map?

Look at this map of the U.S.A. The lakes are blue. Can you find the lakes? How many lakes do you see?

The lakes on the map are big lakes.
The United States has many small lakes too.
There are many places to see in the U.S.A.

Some places have flat land. Lots of
things can grow here.

Some places have sand and rocks.
Not many things grow here.

Some places have big waves. You can find fish and crabs in the water. And you can find shells in the sand.

Some places have many people and lots of cars. The people live in houses and in tall buildings.

See all the places in the U.S.A. Can you find a place like yours?